Jesus is Missing!

ISBN: 978-1-887671-08-8

To all those who meet, greet, welcome, and care for the millions of people who visit Newport, Rhode Island -- the fabulous City-by-the-Sea.

Introduction

It was in the late fall of 2017 that the people of Newport, Rhode Island were busy decorating the city's stores, streetlamps, bridges, and boats in the harbor for the celebration of Christmas.

I was working as a tour guide at the Preservation Society of Newport County, the owner and caretaker of the largest group of Gilded Age mansions in the country. The Society owns eleven historic properties, including nine mansions in Newport and the unique Green Animals Topiary Garden in nearby Portsmouth, Rhode Island. All were built in the late 1800s and early 1900s. The largest and most visited mansions are The Breakers (1895), Marble House (1892), Rosecliff (1902), and The Elms (1901). More than a million people visit each year.

I worked primarily at The Elms, my favorite of all the city's mansions. Each mansion's operation was a team effort. At The Elms, I worked with my colleagues Sam, Suzanne, Priscilla, Carolina, Robin, and Ralph. Jennifer was our team leader. Together, we experienced a memorable Christmas season.

The story that follows is mostly true.

ONE

Christmas Comes to Newport: The City-by-the-Sea

Maybe you remember the winter of 2017. The weather was cold and blustery. Snow was on the ground and more was anticipated. It would be a truly white Christmas. I was working as a tour guide at the Preservation Society of Newport County and was able to see up close all the preparations required for dressing up the society's historic Gilded Age mansions with wreaths, lights, trees, and live poinsettias.

The largest of them all -- The Breakers – was the first to get the Christmas treatment and it was stunning. It featured a towering poinsettia tree in the great hall, multiple lighted trees around the house, decorated fireplaces, thousands of sparkling lights, and a huge electric train display in the upper loggia overlooking the historic Cliff Walk and the Atlantic Ocean. Two other mansions, Marble House and The Elms, would be next to welcome the Society's decorators.

Inside and out, the mansions at Christmas complement the famous City-By-The-Sea's public décor. Lights and decorations wrap around the electric poles and stretch up each historic street and down to the harbor where boats of every description are alive with colored bulbs and evergreen swag.

When the first snow flies, there is no more beautiful place to be. As in past years, Newport's Christmas at the Mansions was going to be an experience to remember. But this year would come with a special twist.

4

TWO

Christmas at The Elms

On Bellevue Avenue, several blocks from The Breakers oceanfront site, is Newport's most elegant mansion, The Elms. This 1901 French chateau was once the summer home of Pennsylvania coal baron Edward Julius Berwind, his wife Sarah, and later, his sister Julia. This majestic two-story 60,000 square foot home, overlooking Newport Harbor, had been the setting for numerous balls and society gatherings for sixty summers.

While the Berwinds never spent a Christmas in The Elms (they lived in Philadelphia), the Preservation Society has each year re-created the spirit of an Elms' Christmas for today's visitors with stunning trees, colorful lights, delicate ornaments, live poinsettias, and displays of antique toys and art from the early 1900s. Oftentimes, a local bakery will create a large lighted model of The Elms from gingerbread and icing to be displayed in the mansion's huge kitchen to the delight of visitors.

Christmas at The Elms also includes the Preservation Society's self-guided and guide-led tours of the mansion's main floors, as well as an intriguing Servant Life Tour that explores the lifestyle and lives of the Berwinds' household staff, many who lived on the Elms' third floor.

THREE

Decorating The Elms

The beginning of the holiday season at The Elms is always marked by the arrival of the mansion's extensive collection of Christmas decorations, strings of white and colored lights, historic toy collections, and artificial wreaths and pine trees. Boxes and boxes of these priceless treasures arrive from the Society's warehouse to be piled carefully in the kitchen area of the great house, staged for the workers and volunteers who annually transform the grand home into a magical wonderland.

The weather made it easy to get in the spirit of the season. It was already snowing when the first boxes of Christmas decorations arrived at The Elms.

The visionary leader of this annual construction is a gentle soul named Jim. For as long as anyone could remember, he has been the decorator and chief designer of the spectacular décor in these Gilded Age mansions. With a small but devoted corps of volunteer elves, he appears each morning in The Elm's grand ballroom to direct the placement of every object in its designated place around the house. As we watched, a half dozen artificial trees were unboxed in the basement staging area just as quickly they were carried off by the mansion's elves to be placed in their respective rooms and salons of the great house.

In just a couple busy weeks, they completely transform the home's spectacular first floor rooms and the second-floor bedrooms, filling them with lights, trees, ornaments, and all the colorful décor of the Christmas season.

One of the most popular attractions in the home is the expansive one-of-a-kind Nativity scene displayed on top of the solid 5,000-pound Italian marble table that dominates the home's second floor landing. The display features some fifty animals and figurines of the merchants, shepherds, and wise men all gathered around Mary, Joseph, and the baby Jesus lying in his manger. It is a focal point for visitors of every age.

FOUR

Setting Up the Nativity

*In those days Caesar Augustus issued a decree that
a census should be taken of the entire Roman
world...And everyone went to their own town to
register. So Joseph went up from the town of
Nazareth in Galilee to Judea, to Bethlehem the town
of David, because he belonged to the house
and line of David.*
-Luke 2:1-4

Perhaps the most interesting Christmas display is the Nativity. At the Elms, the sprawling Christmas Nativity display is set up and the figures carefully arranged on top of the mammoth marble table that greets visitors climbing the staircase to the second-floor landing.

This historic manger scene has long been a focal point of interest for Christmas visitors. They are drawn to the many human figures and the exotic animals, palm trees, and other complementary features. During the Thanksgiving and Christmas holiday season, hundreds of people will respectfully view the display each day and perhaps ponder the meaning of this event some 2,000 years ago.

To even the most casual observer, this Nativity set is unlike any most people have ever seen. It is not fashioned from plaster of Paris, modeling clay, or marzipan like so many of the manger scenes perched on fireplace mantels or tucked under the Christmas trees in homes around the country.

This Nativity has been obviously crafted to be something more, something special, showcasing the work of a talented artist or artists, rendered in resin and hand-painted, with each figure, even the animals, having individual expressions and personalities. There is something mysterious, almost mystical about the look of each of its many pieces. As a whole, it is striking in its artistry and beauty, in the detailed figurines of the people, animals, natural elements, and their presence at the birthplace of Jesus.

When one thinks about this historic event and the written accounts we have from several of the documentarians who captured the scene and described the witnesses and participants, most of us haven't fully imagined what the scene might have actually looked like in those long-ago days. Here, in these figures of people and animals – shepherds, wise men, merchants, goats, camels, cows, caged birds – present at the manger scene with Mary, Joseph, and the baby Jesus, we are given the opportunity to see a more realistic presentation of the scene at the Savior's birthplace.

FIVE

The Nativity: Jesus, Mary & Joseph

*While they were there her days were completed to
give birth, and she bore her first-born Son, whom
she wrapped in swaddling clothes and laid in a
manger, because there was no room for them
in the inn.*
-Luke 2:6-7

At the center of the Nativity one sees the three key figures of
this historic event. We often observe our visitors as they
approach the marble table and its colorful display of green
palm trees, camels and wise men, goats and sheep, cows and
caged birds, and other figures.

Slowly their eyes scan across the layout and they realize it is the Nativity and there at the center of all this posed activity they spy the manger. They often will stop talking and turn quiet as they observe the figures of the gentle and humble Mary and her husband Joseph, caring and marveling over the beautiful baby Jesus lying quietly on his manger bed. It is a most peaceful scene, and many a visitor appears visibly calmer as they continue their visit of The Elms.

SIX

Shepherds & Wise Men Seek Him

> *As the angels went from them into heaven, the*
> *shepherds said to one another, "Let us go straight*
> *to Bethlehem, and let us see what has happened*
> *that the Lord has made known to us." And hastily*
> *they went, found both Mary and Joseph, and saw*
> *the baby lying in the manger.*
> -Luke 2:15-16

The Nativity at The Elms offers visitors a colorful menagerie of animals and their keepers, including the shepherds who had seen the star over Bethlehem while they tended their flocks on the hills outside the town. As related by Luke in the New Testament, an angel of the Lord appeared to the shepherds keeping watch over their flock by night and proclaimed the birth of Jesus, saying "…for today there was born for you in the city of David a Savior, who is Christ the Lord. And this will be a sign to you: You will find a baby wrapped in clothes and lying in a manger." (Luke 2:11-12)

After hearing the words of the angels, the shepherds made their way to the manger to worship the new-born king. King Herod who ruled during this time also wanted to know about this birth and so he called together the Magi who we now know as the three wise men and sent them to Bethlehem to search for the child.

*After listening to the king they travelled on and, lo,
the star they had seen in the east preceded them
until it came and rested above the place where the
young child was. And on observing the star their
joy was boundless. Entering the house they saw the
little Child with His mother, Mary, and prostrating
themselves they worshipped Him. And opening
their treasure chests they offered Him presents:
gold, frankincense and myrrh.*
-Matthew 2:9-11

Most people had never seen figures such as these in a Nativity scene. The animals are exotic and realistic. The clothing and headgear of the Wise Men were stylish, colorful, and appropriate to the times. The faces of the figurines wear the effects of hard work, challenging living conditions, and the long journey they had endured to travel with their gifts for the baby Jesus. Their eyes are calm and respectful. They seem to know they are witnessing something truly and uniquely magnificent.

Little did these witnesses know the scope and impact Jesus' birth would have on the entire world. As that long-ago evening passed, more and more visitors would arrive to see Mary and Joseph and their new baby son.

SEVEN

Jesus Is Missing!

There was nothing to predict what happened next.
It was the middle of a busy Tuesday of Christmas week that December when we heard the voice of Suzanne, the second-floor guide, in our radio earphones. It was one simple sentence, "Jesus is missing!"

Her voice was calm, so calm in fact, that those of us listening from other parts of the house did not initially know what to make of that statement. What was she talking about? How serious was this? Was this a real-time observation? Jesus who? Was it someone's child that was missing? Or was it the little baby Jesus in the manger of the Nativity scene? If so, was he really missing? Had he been taken or stolen? Was he really gone?

Other voices came on the radio. For a moment it was all jumbled, pieces of words, cut off sentences, and fragments as everyone tried to talk and transmit at the same time. Jennifer, the house's team leader finally took charge and asked the pertinent question, "Say again, please."

Suzanne on the second floor responded, "Jesus is missing."
"Okay, Suzanne. Thank you. Now, Jesus who!? Is it somebody's child?"

"No, Jennifer, it's nobody's child. It's Jesus! OUR Jesus!" Suzanne started singing to us over the radio. You know, like 'Away in the manger, no crib for a bed…' Jesus! In the Nativity display!"

"Oh, okay. Please stop singing, Suzanne. I've got it."

"Sorry," Suzanne said.

The team leader spoke again over the radio. "Suzanne, stay there! I'll be right up. Everyone else, look around your area. We're looking for the baby Jesus from our Nativity display. Maybe somebody picked it up. Maybe a child. Keep your eyes open."

A few of us said a silent prayer that Jesus would be found and found soon. Christmas was coming.

Later that day, several posts appeared on social media asking for prayer – "Jesus is Missing! Please pray for His return."

The search was on.

EIGHT

Searching For Jesus

Since learning the previous day's news that Jesus was missing, Elms staff and guides re-traced their steps in a renewed effort to find the missing figurine. All the tour guides acted as if nothing was amiss. But as they walked their rounds, you could see their eyes, slowly panning back and forth, looking for the baby Jesus.

Even in the kitchen, the house mouse, standing by his own tiny tree, was keeping a vigil for Jesus. Elsewhere, prayer warriors all over the state were praying he would be found and returned safely to the manger.

Plans for the next day's Midnight Mass and celebration of Christmas Eve in downtown Newport moved forward, but time was fleeting. The Elms had planned a shorter schedule for Christmas Eve, closing at four in the afternoon.

Co-workers and staff visiting from other mansions whispered their questions to guides with their shared concern -- "Have you found Jesus yet?" and "Is there any news about Jesus?"

On this Christmas week, it seemed everyone wanted to see the Nativity and there were more comments and questions than usual from the guests. Not surprisingly, they were the same two questions the guides had been getting all day -- "Where is Jesus?" and "Did you know the baby Jesus is missing from the manger?"

Publicly, the guides had no comment. Privately, their hearts were aching and praying for a miracle.

NINE

A Christmas Miracle

On the morning before Christmas, the heavy rod iron doors of The Elms were unlocked and opened to welcome the day's first guests. Greetings of "Merry Christmas!" filled the entrance way and echoed off the marble of the soaring staircase.

It was going to be a busy day, a cold winter day. Guests arrived at the front door, bundled in stocking caps, heavy jackets, scarves, gloves, and leather boots. As the home's front door swung open for each new arrival, the guides would feel the biting gust of the frigid weather outside.

Poinsettias, stately decorated trees, and staircases wrapped in evergreen swag greeted the smiling faces. The house was lit with more than two thousand bright white and colored bulbs. The air was filled with the animated excitement of Christmas.

As people filed into the house, the tour guides' radios quietly crackled with directions and comments from the mansion's team leader. One guide asked the question that had been on everyone's mind for the past day, "Has the baby Jesus been found yet?" There was no answer, just silence.

Guides whispered to each other as they passed in the hallways and stairwells. "Did anyone find Jesus?"
"Is Jesus back yet?" "Any news about Jesus?"

As she had responded the day before, the team leader patiently answered the query, "No, but please be on the lookout. We'll get him back."

No one was giving up.

And then it happened.

Like every inexplicable event in the history of inexplicable events, it occurred in a flash. Nobody saw anything, even those who were walking near the marble table on the second floor.

It seems that as suddenly as he had vanished, there he was again.

The baby Jesus just appeared, precious and innocent and joyful, lying between Mary and Joseph on His manger bed. It was Sam who first spotted the baby returned and excitedly whispered the good news over the radio from his second-floor post, "Jesus is back!"

You could hear the voices of every guide coming from every part of the house, from the basement to the third floor, all in unison, shouting as one ---"Yaaaay!!"

A great shout of hallelujah. Unrehearsed. A shout of great joy. A fervent prayer answered. Jesus was back!

Everyone then wanted to know how, who, when. The questions came rapid fire. How did it happen? Who was it? Who had Him? Did you see who brought back Jesus? Was He found somewhere in the house? How did it happen? Good questions. Obvious questions. Questions wanting answers.

Alas, there would be no answer.

Sam had been the guide closest to the Nativity and to the actual return of the baby, but he hadn't seen either a person or a flash of lightning or anything. No one saw anything.

However it happened, it was never discovered. He was missing one moment and in the next moment Jesus was lying again in the manger between Mary and Joseph. Utterly amazing.

Later, to anyone who asked -- and thousands did ask over the following weeks -- the return of the missing Jesus would be simply described by the staff as what it was - a Christmas Miracle.

The End

ABOUT THE AUTHOR

Kenneth Proudfoot is a lifelong writer, playwright, author, teacher, and documentary film producer.

He loves tours and travel and history. He previously led the *Servant Life Tour* at The Elms (Newport, RI), and the *Beneath the Breakers* tours at The Breakers (Newport, RI). He was the former Administrator at the Block Island Historical Society (Block Island, RI), and created and led 3-week college student *Entrepreneurship in Eastern Europe* tours through the Czech Republic, Slovakia, Poland, and Hungary. He has worked and traveled in 52 countries.

His films include *The Amazing Life & Times of Austin T. Levy* (2016), and, with co-producer, Sage Fizacolla, *Allie's Donuts: The Documentary* (2016).

His books include **The Official 2018 Newport Tour Guides & Greeters Handbook** (Shoreline Press (RI), 2017); **Welcome to Wickford** (Wickford Institute, 2016); **Austin T. Levy: Socially Conscious Entrepreneur** (Shoreline Press (RI), 2015); **Why Rhode Island Matters! First in Independence, Industry, Art & Innovation** (Editor, 2010); and **There ARE No Limits!: Thoughts on Embracing the Entrepreneurial Spirit!** (EP Press, 2002).

www.ingramcontent.com/pod-product-compliance
Lightning Source LLC
Chambersburg PA
CBHW041032170626
46815CB00005B/297